A Note to Parents and Caregivers:

Read-it! Readers are for children who are just starting on the amazing road to reading. These beautiful books support both the acquisition of reading skills and the love of books.

 The PURPLE LEVEL presents basic topics and objects using high frequency words and simple language patterns.

 The RED LEVEL presents familiar topics using common words and repeating sentence patterns.

 The BLUE LEVEL presents new ideas using a larger vocabulary and varied sentence structure.

 The YELLOW LEVEL presents more challenging ideas, a broad vocabulary, and wide variety in sentence structure.

 The GREEN LEVEL presents more complex ideas, an extended vocabulary range, and expanded language structures.

 The ORANGE LEVEL presents a wide range of ideas and concepts using challenging vocabulary and complex language structures.

When sharing a book with your child, read in short stretches, pausing often to talk about the pictures. Have your child turn the pages and point to the pictures and familiar words. And be sure to reread favorite stories or parts of stories.

There is no right or wrong way to share books with children. Find time to read with your child, and pass on the legacy of literacy.

Adria F. Klein, Ph.D.
Professor Emeritus
California State University
San Bernardino, California

Editor: Jill Kalz
Designer: Joe Anderson
Page Production: Angela Kilmer
Creative Director: Keith Griffin
Editorial Director: Carol Jones
The illustrations in this book were created digitally.

Picture Window Books
5115 Excelsior Boulevard
Suite 232
Minneapolis, MN 55416
877-845-8392
www.picturewindowbooks.com

Printed in the United States of America.

Library of Congress Cataloging-in-Publication Data
Jones, Christianne C.
Tricia's talent / by Christianne C. Jones ; illustrated by Beatriz Helena Ramos.
p. cm. — (Read-it! readers)
Summary: Tricia tries doing many different things until she finally finds the activity
she is most talented at.
ISBN-13: 978-1-4048-1727-2 (hardcover)
ISBN-10: 1-4048-1727-1 (hardcover)
[1. Individuality—Fiction.] I. Ramos, Beatriz Helena, ill. II. Title. III. Series.
PZ7.J6823Tri 2007
[E]—dc22   2006003417

Tricia's Talent

by Christianne C. Jones

illustrated by Beatriz Helena Ramos

Special thanks to our advisers for their expertise:

Adria F. Klein, Ph.D.
Professor Emeritus, California State University
San Bernardino, California

Susan Kesselring, M.A.
Literacy Educator
Rosemount–Apple Valley–Eagan (Minnesota) School District

PiCTURE WiNDOW BOOKS
Minneapolis, Minnesota

Tricia was a talented girl. She was good at almost everything she tried.

All of her friends had something they did best. Tricia wanted to find her BEST talent.

Her sister played the piano. She was the best piano player.

Tricia tried to play the piano. She practiced for two hours.

Tricia liked playing the piano, but it wasn't her best talent.

Her brother played T-ball. He was the best T-ball player.

Tricia tried to play T-ball. She hit
the ball into the outfield!

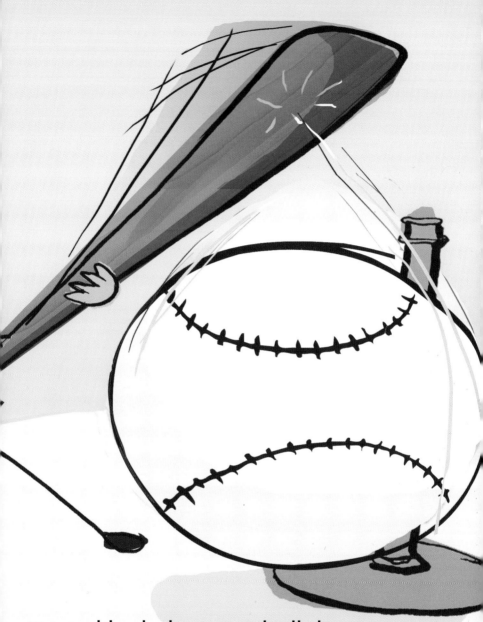

Tricia liked playing T-ball, but it wasn't her best talent.

Her classmates jumped rope at recess.

They were the best rope jumpers.

Tricia tried to jump rope. She jumped
twenty times in a row!

Tricia liked jumping rope, but it wasn't her best talent.

Her best friend ran track. She was the best runner.

Tricia tried to run track. She ran
around the track four times and did
the long jump.

Tricia liked running track, but it wasn't her best talent.

Her dad played the saxophone.
Tricia tried to play the saxophone.
Beautiful notes filled the air.
She loved it! Tricia found
her BEST talent.

More *Read-it!* Readers

Bright pictures and fun stories help you practice your reading skills. Look for more books at your level.

Back to School 1-4048-1166-4
The Bath 1-4048-1576-7
The Best Snowman 1-4048-0048-4
Bill's Baggy Pants 1-4048-0050-6
Camping Trip 1-4048-1167-2
Days of the Week 1-4048-1581-3
Eric Won't Do It 1-4048-1188-5
Fable's Whistle 1-4048-1169-9
Finny Learns to Swim 1-4048-1582-1
Goldie's New Home 1-4048-1171-0
I Am in Charge of Me 1-4048-0646-6
The Lazy Scarecrow 1-4048-0062-X
Little Joe's Big Race 1-4048-0063-8
The Little Star 1-4048-0065-4
Meg Takes a Walk 1-4048-1005-6
The Naughty Puppy 1-4048-0067-0
Paula's Letter 1-4048-1183-4
Selfish Sophie 1-4048-0069-7
The Tall, Tall Slide 1-4048-1186-9
The Traveling Shoes 1-4048-1588-0
A Trip to the Zoo 1-4048-1590-2
Willy the Worm 1-4048-1593-7

Looking for a specific title or level? A complete list of *Read-it!* Readers is available on our Web site:
www.picturewindowbooks.com